·IOI·
DOG STREET

The Story of **AMOS**
THE BUMMED-OUT CANINE

By Shelley Fraser Mickle
with Blake Beckett

Illustrated by Phoebe North

Amos lives at 109 Dog Street. He has lived there nine weeks.

Every day Amos's owners throw him a bone. Then they drive off to work. They leave Amos in the yard alone.

And there Amos is. From dawn to dusk—alone, alone, alone.

Amos is so alone, his teeth itch. He feels so lonely, his ears hang down. They hang down on his head like wet bread. And loneliness sloshes inside of him like a fish tank with no fish.

Amos used to make a list of things he liked.

1. Squirrels
2. Bones

Nothing can be as much fun as a squirrel to chase. And nothing lasts so long as a bone to chew. But lately his list has grown by zero.

And he has started a Hate List that seems to add something every day. So far, his Hate List has:

1. Pain
2. Loneliness
3. Rude squirrels
4. A rude squirrel calling him Bone Head
5. Teeny-tiny bones
6. Fleas between his toes, and
7. Flies on his tail

Amos is bummed out.

He is a bummed-out canine. Bummed out means he is tired and sad. *Canine* is a fancy word for dog. And that is also the only fancy thing about Amos.

And now Amos has grown tired of being sad.

The truth is, Amos was dropped off. It was not his idea to live at 109 Dog Street.

It happened like this. Two years ago, a young man named Ned passed by a basket of puppies.

Ned reached in and pulled out one. That one was Amos.

Ned bought Amos for ten dollars and took him home.

During the day Ned spent a lot of time at college. But in the afternoons he would play with Amos.

And then Ned finished school. He got a job in a faraway city.

"I'll come back for you," Ned said to Amos.

Ned decided to take Amos to his parents' house—109 Dog Street. Dog Street is in the countryside. Ned's parents live on a street with other farm houses.

Many fields and woods are there. And hundreds of squirrels live in the woods.

Maybe thousands.

"You will like it there," Ned said. "You will have lots of squirrels to chase."

Ned drove up to his parents' house with Amos in the backseat.

Ned's parents came out of the house and hugged Ned. They were sorry Ned was moving far away.

Ned said, "So here is Amos. Thanks so much for keeping him." They all three leaned over and looked at Amos in the backseat.

Ned reminded them, "When I get settled, I'll come back for him."

Ned knew his parents didn't much care for dogs. They had ideas about dogs. Dogs drool. Dogs jump up on you. They track dirt in the house. They have fleas. They can chew up your shoes.

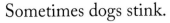

Sometimes dogs stink.

They also tie you down. You can't just drive off on a vacation and leave a dog at home, alone.

Dogs also eat a lot and can run up a grocery bill. And Amos looked like he would eat a lot. More than once when Ned walked down the street with Amos, someone would say, "Wow! Look at that dog! He is the size of a hog."

Amos could blame his looks on his family. His father was a bloodhound. His mother was a poodle. His grandfather was a bird dog. And his grandmother was a Shih Tsu.

Amos is half a hound dog, but so what?

His coat is black. His eyebrows are brown. His tail has a white snip on the end as if he stuck it in a paint can. And sometimes, he *does stink.*

Ned's parents studied Amos in the backseat. They didn't want to hurt Ned's feelings. They didn't want to say that Amos was the ugliest dog they'd ever seen. They didn't want to point out, either, that Amos was drooling all over the backseat.

Amos lifted his eyebrows and looked back at Ned's parents. He was trying to be a good sport. He wanted to make Ned proud of him.

That morning Ned had given Amos a bath. But Amos didn't like the awful shampoo smell. *Humans' noses are so strange!* he thought.

Already Amos was getting a bad feeling about living with Ned's parents. He held up his nose and went *sniff, sniff, sniff*, like a calculator counting numbers.

Amos inherited his nose from his bloodhound father. Ned always likes to say that Amos has the finest nose in the whole fifty United States.

More than once, when Ned lost his ball cap, Amos sniffed it out. That was easy. That ball cap was stinky with ball-game sweat.

Once Amos sniffed out Ned's missing car keys. That was easy, too. They had the smell of Ned's hands on them.

Often Amos sniffed out a fast-food chicken bone thrown away in ditch weeds. And then Amos and Ned would wrestle. It's not safe for a dog to eat a chicken bone. A chicken bone could splinter and stick in Amos's throat.

Amos always fought Ned hard for chicken bones.

Probably Amos fought Ned so hard for chicken bones because Ned did not want Amos to have them. And that made Amos want them even more! But Ned always won.

Now Amos was sniffing out Ned's parents' place. And he did not like what his nose was telling him.

Ned's parents were still looking in the car window at Amos. Their own noses were wrinkled and turned up.

Ned opened the car door. He started pointing out all of Amos's good traits.

"He is...well, if not exactly handsome, shiny at least. He can jump high. He runs after balls. He won't bring them back. But he *will* run after them.

"He can sniff out anything. And he will sleep beside you, all through the night. He will keep you company and watch over you. And he is easy to love."

Ned held out his arms. He looked as if he were about to introduce the star in a show.

"Meet Mr. Amos, one fine canine! He has the finest nose in the whole U.S."

Amos bounded out of the car. He passed Ned's parents.

He nearly knocked Ned's mother down, because his nose told him there was a squirrel behind her. And he was headed straight for it.

He chased that squirrel across the yard.

But then—that squirrel stopped! It turned around and did a hateful thing. It threw a nut at Amos. And it sang,

"Nanny nanny boo boo.
Here's a bone to chew, chew.
You can't catch me, you silly-looking dog.
Come and get it, Bone Head."

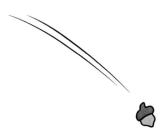

It was a rude squirrel. It was also a lying squirrel.

That squirrel didn't have a bone! Amos could see that its paws were empty. But most of all, Amos hated being called Bone Head.

Amos took off. He chased that rude squirrel up a tree.

The tree limb broke. The limb fell on a garbage can. Crash!

The squirrel took off again.

Amos ran fast. He ran so fast his ears flapped.

Amos wanted to catch that squirrel more than he wanted a soup bone! More than he wanted even a thrown-away dangerous chicken bone!

He wanted that squirrel more than a ham bone. Or a car ride. Or a trip to the beach. Or to roll in something with a sweet stinky smell. And all the while he was hollering, "Ahooo, ahooo, you can't outrun me!"

On all the farms nearby, everyone could hear Amos. His hound-dog father had given him not only his nose but also his voice. Amos could bay like a French horn in a marching band.

Amos jumped over a lawn mower. He crawled under a fence.

He trotted through the garden at 108 Dog Street.

He jumped in the pool at 107. He swam across doing a poodle paddle.

And he ran through the barn at 106.

He shook himself dry at 105.

And he gave up at 104.

That's because 104 is where the rude squirrel climbed an oak tree fifty feet high.

That squirrel was a bad sport. And it was not just a little rude. It was *very* rude.

That squirrel sat up there singing down at Amos,

"You can't catch me.
Silly half-a-hound dog.
But good try! Bone Head."

And it popped Amos right on the head with another nut!

Amos walked back to Ned. His tongue was hanging out. It was hanging out almost to his knees.

That was the first time he'd been called Bone Head. And, wow! He sure hated it. Being called Bone Head was worse than having fleas between his toes.

"Please?" Ned looked at his parents. "What else can I do with Amos?"

"Well, okay," Ned's father said. "But just for a little while."

"We'll make do," Ned's mother said. "But I wonder, will mints sweeten his breath?"

It was true. Amos chewed on bones so often, he often had a bad case of bone breath. He also liked to wash down his bones with toilet water.

Ned drove off.

Now, every day, Amos lies in the yard.

He is more alone than he ever was when he lived with Ned. To pass the time, he chews on bones.

He chews them for so long, they become

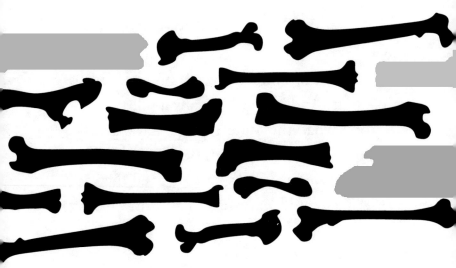

slick and slimy. They drip spit.

He tries to make his bones last from dawn to dusk. But every day he becomes more and more bummed out.

He is even beginning to forget what Ned looks like.

A squirrel teases, sitting on a tree limb.

"Nanny Nanny Boo Boo.
You can't catch me.
You're stuck in the yard.
That's easy to see,"

Sometimes one of those rude squirrels comes right to the edge of the yard. It breathes into Amos's face. Its breath smells like nuts. And its paws are always dirty.

But what the rude squirrel says is true. Amos *is* stuck in the yard. Because soon after Amos moved in, Ned's parents fixed the yard so Amos could never again run off chasing squirrels.

At least he could only run off with great pain. And great pain is always at the top of Amos's Hate List.

This is how it happened.

To keep Amos from running around the neighborhood, Ned's parents hired a company to wire their yard. Two men came in a truck.

They buried a wire in the ground. Then Ned's father put a collar on Amos. It too had a wire in it.

Amos learned not to cross the wire buried in the ground. If he did, the wire in his collar went "Burr" and spit a shock at him.

The shock hurt like thirty bee stings.

Amos could always jump the wire. But nothing seemed worth thirty bee stings.

Soon Amos was stuck in the yard all day until Ned's parents came home. To pass the time, he often chased squirrels up to the wire and then stopped.

And the rude squirrels would sing back,

"You can't catch me,
silly half-a-hound dog.
You can't even try.
By the way, your breath smells like a
hog's behind.
Bone Head, Bone Head, Bone Head!"

Being surrounded by so many rude squirrels was a nightmare. It was making Amos nuts.

Hour after hour, Amos lay in the yard.

Not a thing to do.

Nothing to chase far.

Nobody's nice warm hand to scratch an itch.

He lay around with his feet in the air, or curled in a bow, scratching an itch with his teeth and toes.

When he slept, his legs ran in dreams.

And in his dreams he always chased rude squirrels and caught them!

He made them take back every Bone Head

they'd called him.

He bombarded them with a rat-a-tat of nuts on their heads until they cried,

"Oh, Amos, we're sorry! We love you!"

He also dreamed of Ned.

His dreams started with Ned throwing balls for him to chase. Then Ned would give him bones, and more bones. Soup bones and ham bones. Fat bones and long bones.

And every bone always was juicy.

Then in his dream Ned and Amos would go to the park. There Amos could chase a nice squirrel, one who was a good sport.

Soon his dream would change. Ned would drive away. And Amos would wake up panting.

Every day Amos's Hate List grows. He has moved Bone Head up to number two. Now his list has a total of ten:

1. Pain
2. Being called Bone Head
3. Loneliness
4. Rude Squirrels
5. Baths
6. Breath mints
7. Teeny-tiny bones
8. Fleas anywhere
9. Flies on his tail
10. Rude squirrels dropping nuts on his head

Today Ned's father could not find his truck keys. He ran all over, looking everywhere. "Where are my truck keys? Where are my keys?"

He looked in the laundry basket. He looked behind the cushions on the couch.

He looked in all his pants' pockets. And then, "Oh, Fiddley Futz! I am late. I have to go!"

He jumped in the car beside Ned's mother, who would have to drive him to work. Worst of all, he was supposed to take bats and balls to his softball team's game that night. He really needed his truck.

Ned's mother said, "Maybe you lost your keys walking in the woods yesterday. Maybe that's where we should hunt for them."

"Maybe," Ned's father agreed. "But when I get home it will be nearly dark. I will have to hunt them with a flashlight. I hate letting my team down."

Ned's mother backed out of the driveway. Amos heard over his shoulder a rude squirrel chattering. "Bone Head, Bone Head."

That rude squirrel was calling Ned's father a Bone Head!

Amos turned around and stuck his tongue out at the rude squirrel. But that rude squirrel only said, "What you looking at, Bone Head?"

In all their rush, Ned's parents forgot to throw Amos a bone.

Now Amos lies on the grass. His loneliness feels like his heart is being squeezed. He is so bummed out that he doesn't even feel like digging up the bone he buried yesterday. Amos closes his eyes, trying to sleep.

Suddenly, he hears a voice.

It is a dog voice.

Amos wonders, "Am I dreaming?"

The morning sun is as warm as French toast. Amos sits up.

No longer do his ears lie on his head like wet bread. He turns his head to hear better.

Yes, it is a voice. A real dog voice. It is deep. It is soft. And it is saying, "Hey, big guy. Wanna see something *spectacular*?"

Spectacular?

Spectacular sounds like something you might call a big bone. A really big bone.

Yes, a spectacular bone.

Amos puts up his nose and goes *sniff, sniff, sniff*, like a calculator counting numbers.

He is not about to answer that voice without doing some investigating. He knows about *investigating*. That's what Ned often said. He was going to investigate job openings. And then Ned was gone.

Amos goes to the corner of the yard. He stands as close to the hot wire as he can get. One more step and he'll get zapped.

I'll act like I'm talking to a squirrel, he thinks. *Then if that voice is not really a nice dog, I won't have to talk to him.*

Amos worries that the rude squirrels hired a bear to act like a dog.

Or maybe the squirrels hired a rude dog to trick him.

"If I figure this out," Amos thinks, "then I won't give those squirrels one more chance to call me a Bone Head."

So Amos says, just as if he were talking to a squirrel, "No way. Not today, dumb squirrel. You can't fool me—promising something *spectacular.*"

But the truth is, Amos is so bored that he's ready to go off with almost anyone. He's ready to go off to see almost anything. He just does not want to go off with a bear or a mean dog who will beat him up.

And whomever he breaks out of the yard to see has to be worth thirty bee stings.

Amos feels smart. He is doing a good job of investigating. He lies down and waits for an answer.

In a tree above his head a squirrel is chewing a nut. The squirrel drops the nut on Amos's head. Amos can hear that squirrel saying, "Hee, hee, hee."

Then the deep dog voice comes again. "Come on, Kiddo. Jump the wire. I'll show you something spectacular."

"I'm not sure I want to," Amos says cautiously. He wants to hear the voice more.

Then he can decide if it is
a bear talking like a dog.

"That's silly, Amos,"
the voice says. "How can
you pass up a chance
to see something
spectacular?"

"Where are you?"
Amos calls back.

"Jump the wire. I'll
coach you. I'll tell you
how to find me."

Amos decides the invitation is worth a
chance. But oh, how it will hurt!

He takes a deep breath. He backs up.

He wants a running start.

He closes his eyes. *Will it be worth it? Oh!
I hope it will be worth it. Please, be worth it!*

He holds his breath. He jumps into the
air.

His ears flap. He holds out his legs as if he
might fly. *"EEEyiiii!"* he screams.

He soars across the hidden wire. He lands

on the other side and crosses the street.

"Wow!" he says to himself. "That was more like forty bee stings."

Amos shakes his whole body. He pants hard until the hurting stops.

"I'm here," the dog voice says. "Take twenty-five steps to the right. Then fifteen to the left. And look under the blooming bush."

Amos counts off the steps.

"One
Two
Three
Four
Five
Nine, oops, I mean six,
Seven
Eight
Nine

Ten
Twelve, oops, I mean eleven
Twelve
Thirteen."

He stops. *I better do this right,* he thinks, *or the squirrels will be right: I will be a bone head.*

"Fourteen
Fifteen
Sixteen
Seventeen
Eighteen
Nineteen
Twenty
Twenty-one
Twenty-two
Twenty-three
Twenty-four
Twenty-five
Twenty-six."

"Oops. Did I go one too far?" He steps back and turns left.

"One, two, three, four, five, six, seven, eight,

nine, ten, eleven, twelve, thirteen, fourteen, fifteen, sixteen, seventeen, eighteen. Oh no, I've gotten carried away!" He backs up three steps. And then he arrives at the fence at 107 Dog Street.

The bush has blooming white flowers like stars. It smells like a bee's bank. It smells like a place where lots of blooms are stored.

Suddenly from behind the bush a yellow dog stands up.

Whew! Amos thinks. *It really is a dog. It is not a bear. And it is not a dog to beat me up. At least, it does not look like it wants to beat me up.*

"I'm Jake," the dog says, "and for weeks I've been watching you."

"Yeah?" To Amos, the thought that another dog has been watching him feels nice. It makes his loneliness feel shaved down.

"You're bummed out, Amos. I can see."

"Yeah," Amos says. "My first owner, Ned, said he was bummed out when he had too many tests at school. And now he is gone.

And I'm bummed out."

"It's never a good idea to be sad for long. That's why you need to see something spectacular."

Amos looks at Jake. Amos sees what, at first, he did not see. The dog is a Labrador retriever. He is a purebred. Of that, Amos is sure.

Amos figures that Jake must have once been very handsome. He may have even won ribbons in a show ring. He is certainly a spectacular canine.

But Jake's eyes are now glazed over. They look like old scratched marbles. They are as dark as wet nuts.

"Come on, we've got to get going if we're going to get there," Jake says in dog-talk.

"Where?"

"Where I told you. To see something spectacular. First, though, you have to dig me out. Look, I have a hole started. I just can't seem to finish it."

Beside the bush, under the fence, is half a hole.

Amos starts digging.

Jake lies beside the hole. "You see," he says, "over the years I've gotten a bit fat. I started out here as a pup. Two little girls got me as a gift. But then the girls grew up. They have cars of their own now. Sometimes they still let me sleep beside them. But I have a problem."

"What problem?" Amos asks.

"I roll in things. Things that smell bad. Well, the girls think the things smell bad. But they smell good to me. Things like cow manure. And horse poop. And oh, yeah, anything dead. By the way, I love your breath. Was that a soup bone you had this morning? Or a rib?"

"I had a bone yesterday," Amos says. "Actually two—a soup bone and a rib. But I buried the soup bone for later. But today I didn't even feel like digging it up."

Jake now crawls into the hole that Amos has dug. Lying on his stomach, Jake scoots under the fence. He comes out the other side. He stands up panting.

Jake is still talking. "To tell you the truth," he says, "I can't remember how old I am. It has a one in it, I'm sure. And maybe a two. Or is it a three? Oh, I can't remember!"

Now Jake is walking down the street leading Amos.

Jake's legs are stiff. They look like ax handles that can barely move.

Jake's toenails scrape the pavement. And his tail sags. When he turns his head to talk to Amos, he moves like a wooden doll that creaks.

"But Amos, do you know what I hate more than not knowing how old I am?" Jake asks.

"What?" Amos replies.

"Losing my puppy ways. I used to like nothing better than chasing my tail. Now that seems stupid.

"I used to like to wrestle. Now that hurts. And run after balls. Oh, what's the use? And swim. Now I can't get out of the pool. And that leaves…Well, do you know what I do all day?"

"What?" asks Amos.

"I have a list. It's called the Today List. And I do it every day.

1. **Sleep**
2. **Eat**
3. **Nap**
4. **Move around, but only a little**
5. **Nap**
6. **Try to sniff out something stinky**
7. **Find it**
8. **Roll in it**

9. Feel sorry I did it
10. Watch the kids come home
11. Sleep

"Sometimes along the way I get a bath. Sometimes instead I get shut in the barn for the night. And you know what is really bumming me out? I'm starting to think my nose is broken. I can't smell what I used to."

Amos walks beside Jake. He keeps his feet slow so he and Jake can be side by side.

"My nose smells out too much," Amos says. "It can drive me nuts. Bones here, squirrels there, loneliness everywhere. If I weren't wired in, I'd be following my nose all over the world.

"I also have a Hate List," Amos admits. "And it keeps growing. But I think right now, it might be changing."

The morning sun moves well into the sky. The pavement is as warm on Amos's paws as a roasted bone.

With Jake beside him, Amos feels Loneliness falling down on his Hate List. It won't ever fall all the way off his Hate List, he knows.

But right now, the pain of loneliness has lost its sting.

Suddenly Jake grabs Amos's neck with his teeth. He gives him a great tug.

A car speeds out of the driveway at 105.

The car's tires miss Jake and Amos—barely. "You've got to watch out for cars," Jake says, letting go of Amos. He spits out a little of Amos's hair. It was stuck on his teeth.

Jake's teeth are yellow with age. And one tooth is cracked from when he retrieved a golf ball.

Behind them, a little white dog is digging out from under the fence. The dog looks like a jelly roll on sticks.

"That's Miss Lucy," Jake says as the little dog runs after the car.

"She hates being left behind. But her chances of catching her owner's car are about one hundred to one. And one hundred to one are not good odds."

"Shouldn't we help her?" Amos watches after Miss Lucy. "What if she runs so far she gets lost?"

"Oh, she'll give up in a minute and come back." Jake blows his nose. "Brrrrrr." Then he sneezes, "Ah-chew!" He sees Miss Lucy stop in the street.

"She's got a lot of terrier in her," Jake says. "Her heart is bigger than her brain. She can't tell trouble even when it licks her."

Jake goes on walking. He knows Miss Lucy will catch up.

And soon she does.

Lucy arrives, panting. She walks between Amos and Jake. She is no bigger than a cat. A fat cat. She is prissy, too.

"What you need to do is chew on a cedar stick," Lucy says to Amos. "Then your breath won't smell so bad to humans. And Jake, you'd better stop rolling in cow manure. It's the hardest to get off."

Amos has never been around dogs who like to talk so much. Before they get to 104, Lucy has named all the things she likes to chase. And a lot of them are right there in the neighborhood:

"1. Rabbits
2. Lizards
3. Any other dog
4. Any other dog with a bone who will not share
5. Bikes
6. Balloons
7. Cats
8. Pickup trucks with fat tires
9. Pickup trucks with skinny tires
10. Red pickup trucks
11. Blue pickup trucks
12. Pickup trucks of any color
13. Rude squirrels."

"By the way," Miss Lucy asks, "where are we going?"

"To see something spectacular," Amos says.

"What?"

But Amos can't answer. He doesn't know. And he doesn't care. He is along for the walk. And he is so in love with being with Miss Lucy and Jake that seeing something spectacular no longer matters. He's glad he jumped the wire.

"I got loose last week and saw it for

myself, "Jake says. "It's at 101. And it is truly spectacular."

From the yard at 103, a squirrel sprints across the road. It runs up a tree and starts throwing nuts at Amos and Miss Lucy. That rude squirrel calls them Bone Heads. Even Chicken Bone Heads!

Amos and Lucy take off after the rude squirrel quicker than you can say, "No spaghetti for you today."

Amos and Lucy's claws scrape the tree trunk.

Everybody knows dogs can't climb trees. Especially squirrels know.

That rude squirrel sings down at Amos and Lucy,

"Nanny nanny boo boo,
you two are coo coo.
You can't catch me. I am free.
So give up, Bone Heads."

Privately, Jake thinks the squirrel is right. Amos and Lucy should give up. Chasing squirrels is useless. But chase a ball—well, chasing a ball is another thing, indeed.

But Jake doesn't say what he thinks. He doesn't want to hurt his friends' feelings.

Besides, down the road at 101 is something more spectacular than chasing rude squirrels. And Jake is pretty sure that Amos and Lucy will agree. All he has to do is show them.

But at 102 Dog Street, Lucy sees a bull. And she is after it quicker than you can say, "We don't even have any spaghetti today."

The bull is in a pasture close to the street. In two seconds flat, Lucy has slid under the fence and is barking at the bull.

Oh, what terrible things she is saying to it! Things worse than Bone Head.

"Now, just what do you think?" she asks the bull. "Putting yourself on display so close to the street? Flies on your back! Mud on your tail! Drool on your lips!"

Before she is done, Lucy even calls the bull a "Bone-headed Slobbering Fatso!"

Jake turns to Amos. "See what I said about Lucy not seeing trouble? Even when it licks her?"

Jake is right. The bull is now reaching down to lick Miss Lucy on the face. In another second, the bull could bite Miss Lucy's head off.

The bull could even trample Miss Lucy until she is no longer Miss Lucy. The bull is pawing. Dust flies up.

"Quick, Amos!" Jake cries. "Scoot under the fence and save Miss Lucy!"

Amos can't get through the fence. He tries hard. But he is too fat. He is too tall. But his nose sniffs out a fox hole right on the fence line. No fox is in it.

Amos digs the fox hole bigger. He puts his stomach in the hole and scoots under the fence.

Miss Lucy is still teasing the bull. She is making him feel like dirt. And she can't seem to stop!

"Why didn't you comb your hair this morning? And brush your teeth? Look at your nose! It's dripping like a hose. You smell so bad, only a buzzard could love you."

Amos runs in circles.

He goes around the bull. Around and

around. He runs and barks, "Step back, Bone Head! Back! Back!"

Then Amos thinks it is probably not a good idea to call a bull a Bone Head. Miss Lucy has already enraged the bull by all she's called him.

So now Amos barks softer. "I should warn you, Mr. Bull. You are handsome. A very handsome bull. And that little dog, Miss Lucy, looks like a jelly roll on four sticks. But she's got worms. A bad case of worms. If you lick her again, you yourself might get a painful case of worms!"

Miss Lucy stops. "Amos! How dare you!"

Amos lowers his head. "Sorry. But I want to save you, Miss Lucy. And it's all I can I think of."

Suddenly the bull stands still, frozen by the fear of a painful case of worms.

Amos and Miss Lucy scamper off.

Back on the safe side of the fence, Lucy licks Amos's lips. "I forgive you," she says, and then, "Yum. Did you have soup bone for breakfast, or rib?"

"Rib," Amos says, pleased. Then he remembers that morning. Ned's parents had forgotten his bone.

Just talking about bones puts them on Miss Lucy's mind. "You hungry?" she asks Amos.

"I'm always hungry," Amos admits.

"I could use a little snack," Jake says.

Jake's idea of a snack is a ten-pound bag of dog food. Or a picnic table full of food when a rainstorm comes. Because that's when humans are likely to run off, leaving all the picnic to him.

"Yum," Jake daydreams. "Hamburger, chicken salad, fried chicken, tuna fish, peanut butter." Jake's nose is doing a wiggle dance.

Miss Lucy sniffs in the ditch beside the street. She disappears in the thick weeds.

She burrows down. The ditch weeds look like they are in the middle of a wind storm as she moves through. Amos is right beside her, sniffing out what is in that ditch.

His nose tells him that at some time in the night, a field mouse passed through. And a frog, and a turtle, and a snake, and…

Jake lies beside the street and watches Miss Lucy and Amos sniff out all the trails.

"Oh, joy!" Miss Lucy suddenly yelps. She scurries out of the ditch with a bag in her teeth.

It is a take-out chicken-dinner bag. She scratches it open. She roots inside.

She pulls out a drumstick bone and holds it in her teeth. Some human has eaten it clean. But a little meat is on the end.

"Oh, joy. Oh, joy!" Amos barks. He also puts his head in the bag. Then he hears Miss Lucy's teeth cracking her bone.

The sound reminds him of a chicken bone in his own teeth. And it comes back to him: the way Ned always wrestled chicken bones away from him.

Ned never wrestled anything away from Amos unless it was bad for Amos. There was that time when he was a puppy and he kept biting a lamp cord until Ned wrestled it away from him.

Ned said that lamp cord would have shocked Amos's lips worse than thirty bee stings. He wouldn't have been able to eat puppy food for days—his lips would have been so sore.

Amos whirls around. "No!" he yells in bloodhound. He yips and growls. He jumps on Lucy and wrestles her to the ground. He pulls the chicken bone out of her teeth.

"There you go again!" she yips. "You rude half-a-hound dog! If you weren't three times my size, I'd bloody your nose. I'd tie you in a bow. I'd body-slam you to the ground and knock your head in like a rotten pumpkin, and…"

"Chill out, Miss Lucy," Jake barks. "Don't say anything you'll regret later."

Amos takes the chicken bone back to the ditch. Deciding to bury it, he puts it deep in the soft mud. He pushes mud over it with his nose.

He then trots back to Lucy. "Those chicken bones can kill you! Don't ask me how. Don't ask me why. But I know you shouldn't have one. And all I want to do is save you."

"Oh, that again." Miss Lucy tilts her head. "*Save me! Save me!* You always want to save me. Well, you just saved me from the most delicious lunch I've come across in two days!"

Amos hangs his head. Miss Lucy's words hurt so bad, he feels as if he is bleeding.

In a low, soft voice Amos mumbles, "Miss Lucy, the truth is, I love chicken bones. I love them more than almost anything. More than rib bones. More than beef bones. More than squirrel bones. More than rude squirrel bones. That is, if I ever had the chance to eat rude squirrel bones."

He then says louder, "My darling Ned never lets me have them. He says they can kill me. So if I weren't telling the truth, I would have kept that chicken bone for myself. That is, if I didn't care for you—so much."

Miss Lucy stares at him. She sniffs. Then she reaches up and licks him again. "Oh, Amos, I know. I know now you are telling the truth. I'm sorry I didn't believe you at first. And thank you. You have saved me, once again."

She snuggles up to him. She says in her terrier talk. "I like you. I can even measure how much I like you":

**"More than a rubber-squeak toy
Or a new plaid collar
Or a red sweater
Or a car ride
Or a walk in the park
More than catching a red truck
Or a blue truck
Or...well, you get the idea.**

"I even like you more than the taste of a fast-food chicken bone. Well, maybe.

"Yes, definitely. I like you more than any bone in the world."

"Hurry up!" Jake calls. He is now far down the street. And he is trotting as fast as he can.

15

There is a pickup truck at 101 Dog Street. It is parked in front. There are two horses in the pasture. A cat sits on a fence post. It is licking its paws as if it has just had a snack.

Jake does his scrape-toe walk through the front gate. He does a stiff-legged trot. His nose grows to twice its size.

"Ah, bacon," Jake says. "Eggs too. I don't much care for the strawberries they serve here, but the other stuff is pure heaven."

Amos lifts his nose and smells it all. All of it smells good.

"Heaven!" Lucy cries. "Someone is home here! I can smell him. No. It's a her."

"It's also them." Jake points with his nose to the corner of the house. "Get ready for something spectacular!"

Two puppies wrestle in the grass. They are play-growling. They roll on the ground like two rubber balls stuck together. One is black; one is yellow.

They roll against the porch and break apart. Then they stand up and see Jake. He calls their names. "Hello, Gussie Louise," he says to the black puppy. To the yellow one he says, "Good morning, Pickles."

Suddenly Gussie Louise and Pickles jump on Jake. They jump on him as if he is their long-lost father, home from a hunt.

Pickles leaps up to kiss Jake's lips. Gussie Louise hugs his neck and throws him to the ground.

Jake laughs an old, deep dog laugh. "Ho, ha. And all that."

The puppies jump on Jake again and wrestle with him. He barks with joy, and his stiff old legs wave in the air as if they are laughing.

To Amos and Miss Lucy, Jake calls, "I told you I would show you something spectacular." He gasps as the puppies tickle him.

Lucy—too prissy to roll—lifts her chin. "Hump!" Pickles grabs her tail and up-ends her. Miss Lucy now looks like a jelly roll hidden in grass.

"Jake!" a voice cries from the side of the house. "Is that you? Is it really you, Jake, come to visit again? Well, if it *is* you, I'm happy as a doodle-bug in clover. Happy as a barefoot goat in a box of noodles!"

The voice is followed by a whizzing sound, like wind in grass. Or like tree branches in a rain.

Jake barks a warning. "Here comes Tessee! All tails aside!"

He curls his tail just as a girl sitting on big wheels flies around the corner of the house. Her wheels swerve to miss Jake's tail in the grass. Lights on her wheels flicker with her speed. Her arms turn the wheels in short pushes like jog steps.

Jake warns in a barking voice, "Tessee, you'd better slow down! You know what you'll get."

Tessee seems to understand Jake's bark. She whizzes to a stop, and her lights go out. "Yes, Jake, right you are! You're always right. Right Jake. Bright Jake. How about a piece of cake, Jake? By the way, how are you today?"

Tessee tilts her head as if she will understand exactly what Jake's bark will say. Puppy Pickles comes close to her for a pat.

"Whew!" Jake looks over at Amos and Miss Lucy and Gussie Louise and Pickles. "Last time I was here, Tessee missed running over my tail by barely an inch. I just can't move as quickly out of the way as I used to.

"Last week her mother parked her on the porch for five minutes, saying, 'Now, Tessee, this is for your own good.'

"That's what Tessee gets when she's broken some rule. Instead of *Time Out* she gets *Lights Out*. Tessee had hitched her chair to the lawnmower. She wanted to see if it could pull her faster. Tessee is in love with speed."

Tessee pats Jake's head. His tongue drools on her wheels. She reaches into a bag tied onto her chair. She pulls out a piece of dog cake and gives him some.

Tied onto her chair too are a number of other things:

A flashlight
A hammer
A pair of wire pliers
And a silver horn with a bulb on the end to squeeze

"Oh, Jake," Tessee says, "I'm glad— so glad you came to visit. And who, now just who all is with you?" She holds her hand out toward Amos.

Amos is afraid of the chair with lights. He lowers his head and backs away.

Tessee wheels closer. She touches Amos's collar to read his name. "Oh, Amos, Amos. Welcome, Amos. I see who you are. You are dressed like Gussie in a business suit—all black and brown and brown and black."

Amos smiles. He loves the way Tessee talks, like a slow waltz on the radio. She even puts in a few extra steps, which gives him double the time to understand what she says.

Tessee holds her nose. "Oh, yuck, Amos! Yuckety yuck. P.U.! And double P.U.! What'd you have for lunch? You have the most terrible, most awful—yes, most stinky bone breath I have ever smelled!"

Amos wags his tail. He is so hungry for friends and voices and fun and play. And

Tessee's voice is as warm as French toast. He moves closer and licks her hand.

But Amos has no longer than a minute before Gussie bonks Amos on the head. And she takes off, barking, "Watch me circle this tree. Come on, come on, you can't catch me!" Tessee wheels, following until the lights on her wheels flicker like the lights on a Christmas tree.

Gussie leads Amos in circles. Amos falls over, dizzy. "Oh," he pants, "let me catch my breath. But, oh my!"

Yes, Amos thinks.

Seeing Jake play. Hearing him laugh. The way the puppies remind all of them of their puppy ways—this is totally spectacular!

Amos lies in the grass and catches his breath. The bee stings from the wire—all have been worth this. Very much worth this.

Tessee wheels across the yard and into a field. "Come on, Come on. Let's take a spin. Down to the woods. We'll circle more trees." She wheels down a path.

The puppies leap ahead. Jake trots behind. Miss Lucy and Amos dog trot beside the wheeling lights. "I'm glad you're along," Lucy says to Amos.

As they get near the woods, Tessee looks up and cries, "Oh, no! I forgot about the baby hawks! They just hatched. And look there."

Tessee points to a huge mother hawk—all
brown and gold. The mother hawk has left the
nest, where her babies are. She is now flying
over Tessee and the dogs.

The mother hawk's cry is a like a scream—
Yeiiii, Yeiiii! Her claws look like needles. She
begins circling over Tessee.

"The puppies! The puppies!" Tessee cries.

Jake looks up and barks, "Yes, Tessee, the hawk will steal the puppies! Oh, my!" The father hawk dives toward Pickles.

"The hawks can pick up the puppies!" yells Tessee. "They can take them back to their nest. They can make of them a hawk lunch!"

Jake barks. Amos barks too. He is too big for the hawks to pick up. But Miss Lucy might be just right for a hawk snack!

Miss Lucy sticks her head in the grass. She thinks that if her head is out of sight, the rest of her won't be seen.

Suddenly the father hawk dive-bombs on puppy Pickles's head.

"*Eeeyiii!*" Pickles screams.

The mother hawk dive-bombs on Miss Lucy's rear, which is sticking up.

"*Eiiyiii!*" Miss Lucy screams and takes her head out of the grass. She yells bad, ugly things to that hawk.

The father hawk's talons look like spikes. They look like a fork ready to stick into Pickles and Miss Lucy.

Amos barks low with his bloodhound voice. He jumps and barks. He wants more than anything to scare off the hawks. But what can he do?

Jake shakes his head, so worried he cannot move.

Tessee puts on her brakes. She reaches around on her chair. She unclips her horn and holds it in the air. She squeezes the bulb on the end. The horn blasts the loudest noise Amos has ever heard. It is like a siren, like 1,000 bloodhounds crying all at once.

It blasts, "*Eeee honk! Eeee honk!*"

The hawks shoot straight up into the air. They take off as if they have been shot with a hose.

Tessee keeps squeezing her horn. The hawks dart back into the woods. And now Amos knows what he can do. He lets out his loudest bloodhound cry. He puts his nose to the ground and runs into the woods after the hawks. He will make sure they stay there until the puppies and Miss Lucy are safely back in the yard.

Amos bays like the loudest French horn in a marching band. He runs until the hawks are high up in a tree, sitting near their nest. The baby hawks' heads stick up out of the nest like feather balls.

And right under that tree, Amos stumbles. Something is caught on his toe.

He looks down at his paw. *Sniff, sniff, sniff.*

Somewhere he's smelled that smell before. Oh yes. That's the smell of Ned's father's hands. Right there are the keys, the keys to the truck that Ned's father needs!

Amos picks the keys up with his teeth and trots back to Tessee.

"Hey, Amos, look what you found!" she says, but when Tessee reaches for the keys, Amos will not give them up. He clamps his teeth on them tightly like a snapping turtle.

"Well, okay, then," Tessee says, "they must be really important."

But after another moment, Amos walks up to Tessee's chair and drops the keys in her lap. He knows he can trust her to keep them. And he can't run around wrestling with the puppies with keys in his mouth!

Tessee seems to understand just what Amos means, and she puts the keys in her pocket. "Well, okay then, I'll keep them safe for you, Amos, until you want them back. But whew, that was quite an adventure! Adventure, it was. Puppies, you need to stay close to me. Until you are bigger, you must stay close to me."

She leads them all back into the yard. Jake turns toward the house. "I need a cold drink," he says. "All that has worn me out." He laps water from a bowl on the porch.

Soon all five dogs stick their noses against the glass door at 101. There they see a woman sitting at a desk. Her fingers tap on a keyboard. She is so busy she does not look up.

"What's she doing?" Amos asks.

"I'm not sure," Jake says. "But day after day, she is here. Just like this. Always home. She's writing a story, I think."

"I want to be in it." Lucy scratches on the glass.

"Not likely." Tessee says, from her chair behind them. "She writes mostly about squirrels."

"Rude squirrels, I hope," Amos says. "And I also hope she names one of them Bone Head."

Amos makes a sound like a sneeze. Then he adds, "This morning I would have said that only rude squirrels have all the luck. But now..."

Amos knows no one can call him a bummed-out canine any longer.

The sun sinks. Dusk moves across the fields. The woods look as if a gray cotton blanket has floated down over them.

Cars pull into the driveways at 109 and 108. Then, all the way down the street, car lights turn into driveways. Everyone is home.

Amos sees Jake and Miss Lucy giving the puppies a last lick of a kiss.

Tessee pats her lap, and the puppies jump up for a ride.

Amos goes to Tessee and puts his head on her lap. He licks her pocket.

"Oh, so now you want your keys, Mr. Amos?" Tessee says, "Is that what you're saying, Amos with the bloodhound voice as loud as my horn? Well, okay, Mr. Amos— famous nose Amos—here are your keys."

Amos picks them up and starts to trot home. Or at least to the home where Ned dropped him off.

And as he does, he counts. This time, he counts his list of things he loves from the bottom up:

"5. Bones
4. Nice squirrels
3. Bulls easy to scare
2. 101 Dog Street. AND
1. Friends."

Tomorrow he will dig up that soup bone. The one he buried. And he will give it to Miss Lucy.

He now knows that it is much more fun to love something together than to hate something together.

All spectacular canines figure that out. Even the ones rude squirrels call Bone Head.

epilogue

But that night, Amos did not walk home. Instead, the woman at 101 loaded Jake and Lucy and Tessie with Pickles and Gussie Louise into the back of her truck, and she put Amos in with the others.

She dropped Lucy off at 105. She dropped Jake off at 107.

At 109, she found Ned's parents worried out of their minds. They thought they had lost Amos forever.

And then Amos dropped the keys in front of Ned's father, who picked them up. He looked at Amos with delight and wonder. "My, my! Amos, my boy! Look what you have found! Truly, your nose is as fine as Ned said it was. I do believe you have the most spectacular nose in the whole United States. Now I can get to my ball game on time. Oh, Amos, thank you! Thank you!"

Ned's father hugged Amos. Ned's mother gave Amos a kiss on the top of his head—yes, the same head that rude squirrels had been saying was a bone head!

And then Ned's parents admitted that when they thought they had lost Amos forever, they found they didn't want to live a second longer without him. He had become so easy to love!

Yes, that's what they said.

They said that they knew Amos was not really handsome. But he never lost his shine. They said he liked to put his nose in their laps while they watched TV. He liked to sit beside them when they read the paper. And that made them feel spectacular.

Yes, that's what they said.

They also said that he didn't smell so bad, either— if he had a bath every once in a while. And Amos only drank out of the toilet bowl twice a day now.

They even said that they didn't want to give Amos back to Ned when he came for him. And they were planning to take him on their next vacation. Their only trouble was, they couldn't spend every day with him. They had to work, and they were sorry Amos had to spend so much time alone.

"Well then," said the woman from 101, "let Amos spend the day with me and with Tessee. It seems all dogs need a job. And Amos can babysit my puppies. He can run my doggie day care."

So that's how it is now at 101.

A sign on the street reads:

101 Dog Street, Doggie Day Care
Amos—Director
Jake—Coach
Miss Lucy—Head of Charm
Star puppies—Pickles and Gussie Louise
Mode of transportation—Tessee with the
**   lighted wheels**
Today, accepting more. Apply inside.

So if any time soon you walk down Dog Street and see Amos, you would never call him sad. You would never call him tired. And you would certainly not say he is bummed out.

The squirrels, though, still tease him, calling him Bone Head. But Amos doesn't care, at least not quite so much.

Amos's friends call him other things to make up for the rude squirrels' teasing.

His friends say he is:

1. **Wonderful**
2. **Kind**
3. **Nice smelling**
4. **Quick to share**
5. **The owner of the finest nose in the U.S. and even Canada.**
6. **Able to wrestle a chicken bone out of your mouth quicker than you can say, "We have no spaghetti today."**
7. **Amos is the best friend a dog could ever have.**

HINT: Hold this page upside down in front of a mirror.

the end

Just for Fun

Make up a song using any of the dogs' lists.

But especially make up a song using Miss Lucy's list measuring how much she likes Amos.

Make a rhyme using Jake's Today List.

Make a Puppy Poem.

Make a rap that the rude squirrels could use to tease Amos.

Draw a map from Amos's house to 101 Dog Street.

SHELLEY FRASER MICKLE

Shelley Fraser Mickle is the author of eight other books, including *Barbaro, America's Horse* for children. She lives in Alachua County, Florida, and is the mother of two grown children.

·IOI·
AUTHOR

BLAKE BECKETT

Blake Beckett graduated from Wellesley College and received a Masters of Arts in Reading and Writing at the University of Colorado at Denver. She is Reading Recovery Certified and has taught first or second grade for twelve years. She and her husband, Brian, are the parents to two young children, Bryce and Bailey, and are looking forward to the day when Bryce and Bailey read this book to them.

·101· ILLUSTRATOR

PHOEBE NORTH

Phoebe North is a writer and illustrator from Gainesville, Florida. She earned her Masters of Fine Arts in poetry from the University of Florida in 2009. Her work has appeared in *Umbrella, 2river, Night Train*, and *Mimesis*, among others. She lives with her fiancé, her ukulele, and her tabby cat, Sammy.